The Guinea Pigs

Written by Paul Shipton
Illustrated by Trevor Dunton

In the cage.

In the garden.

In the car.

In the park.

In the car.

11

In the cage.

The Guinea Pigs

:paw: Ideas for guided reading :paw:

Learning objectives: use knowledge of texts to retell to others, recounting main points in correct sequence; identify and write initial and final sounds in CVC words; track text in the right order, developing early directional strategies; use illustrations to predict interest words; explore familiar themes and characters through improvisation and role-play

Curriculum links: Knowledge and Understanding of the World; Citizenship: animals and us

High frequency words: in, the

Interest words: cage, garden, car, park

Word count: 18

Resources: small whiteboards and pens

Getting started

- Ask the children if they own any pets, and what type of pets they own.
- Focus the discussion on guinea pigs. *What do they look like? Where do they live? What do they eat?*
- Go on to discuss what pets do at night when their owners are asleep.
- Discuss the front cover. *Where do you think these guinea pigs are going?*
- Leaf through the book telling the story as you go along. Support the childrens' predictions by saying *and then what happens?*

Reading and responding

- Ask the children to read aloud to p13. As they read, prompt and praise moving from left to right, correct matching of written and spoken words and using a variety of cues.
- When you have finished, encourage the children to read through again independently using finger-pointing.
- Using pp14-15 encourage the children to tell the story in their own words.